Christian

By Dennis O. Hendry

Edited by Vivienne A. Thibodeaux

ISBN: 978-0-9894697-6-0

For the Muskegons

To many, Christian is an evil man; a frustrated, angry, restless soul who shows no mercy on his adversaries.

To Aricka, Christian is her father, however imperfect.

This is a story of a dichotomy between revenge, anger, and great suffering; and how forgiveness, atonement, and purity of heart bring redemption.

TABLE OF CONTENTS

Prologue

Aricka could barely sit still in the car as she had made it back to the house. She had tried nearly her whole life to keep from coming here. To no avail, she still found herself here anyway. It brought thoughts of joyful, fun times along with thoughts of endearing times she would treasure each day since that fateful day her dad didn't come home. That was truly a hard day for her. It was a day she kept tucked away in another part of her memory; a part of her memory which took too much energy to come to terms with. She could remember, like it was yesterday, each moment she had with her dad. It was coming here that would surely bring tears to her face. She knew just being here would bring back all the memories in a vivid recall.

Part One

Chapter One: Carolina

In the beginning
Good always overpowered the evils
Of all man's sins...
But in time
The nations grew weak
And our cities fell to slums
While evil stood strong
In the dusts of hell
Lurked the blackest of hates
For he whom they feared
Awaited them...
Now many, many lifetimes later
Lay destroyed, beaten, beaten down
Only the corpses of rebels
Ashes of dreams
And blood stained streets
It has been written
"Those who have the youth
Have the future"
So come now, children of the beast
Be strong
And SHOUT AT THE DEVIL

-Motley Crue, "In the Beginning", 1983

3

A moment's drive seemed to pass by obliviously and hauntingly slow. The pizza nestled in its stay-warm pouch sat on the passenger seat. Only the friction between its designed bottom and the seat fabric kept it from sliding onto the floor in the quick turns. The pothole ridden streets were something to avoid or to be avoided. The car whined incessantly as its maintenance had been truly lacking. The pizza delivery guy was nearly sweating bullets as he realized this delivery was not on his normal route. He had no time to get lost. He was late and the pizza was surely going to be cold. His customer would surely be upset; hence he would probably not get a tip on this one. Why did he volunteer to deliver this one? He should have told the old timer to do his own delivery, but the old timer was adamant about not doing this one. He said no way; he was not going near that house again. He gave no explanation, but he was truly not going to deliver it; no way, no how.

Ed was the nice guy. He had always taken up any stray order. He knew the franchise would not be rated well if they didn't deliver every pizza. He was the naive delivery guy who could still believe in the honor of the corporate franchise goals. He adeptly maneuvered his little over-used car down the pothole ridden streets as he bumped tirelessly around the corner to the house at 3860 Carolina Street. He knew where it was, but he had never been in this neighborhood. It wasn't his normal route, but it was no problem for him. He could find it.

The car made its last turn. Down the street on the left, he saw the house. He pulled into the front gravel parking area alongside the street. He really liked these types of lots because he could park quickly, get the delivery done, and move on. He put the car in park and grabbed the pizza box out of the heat sleeve. It was getting late. The day was turning into a quiet, thick dusk. He was weary as he wondered if the person waiting inside was going to chew him a new one. He was ready with an apologetic story about his hard time finding the house. He glanced up as he walked to the house on the well-worn sidewalk. He could see someone standing in the window, seemingly waiting for the pizza delivery. He knew this wasn't going to be good.

Oh well, he thought. He had seen worse. He walked onto the porch stoop with a growing concrete crack along the side of the house. He knew these types of porches well because they were all over the city. They were simple, adequate steps poured back during the early fifties housing boom. Everyone working in the mills was building small, bungalow, first time homeowner houses. It was the heyday of everyone having a good paying job and a small new starter house.

He reached out to ring the doorbell, a new stick on type that didn't require wires. Someone must have put this one on quickly to give the tenant the welcoming feeling of a doorbell. It rang sweetly as he stepped to the back of the concrete step to wait for someone to come and open the door. These old houses had screen doors that opened out, so he knew from past trouble to stand on the back of the step to not get hit when they opened it or else risk an awkward delivery around the screen door.

It seemed someone was home, but he didn't hear anyone coming towards the door. He jostled around to peer in the front window to see the guy he saw before in the window. No one was standing there. He started thinking maybe they didn't hear the bell. He surely didn't want to ring the bell again as it would most likely just make them mad. He was already late with their order, but they would just get madder if he tried to get their attention that he was there already. He would wait another minute, but he was very fidgety. He rechecked the receipt to verify the address and looked at the mailbox to make sure they matched. It was a match. He was at the right place.

He was repositioning his hand under the pizza box just as he reached for the doorbell when the handle turned. The door opened quickly while a lady came from around the edge of the door. She was a young, middle aged black woman, apparently in her late thirties. She was well dressed and giddy happy.

"Oh, I hope I didn't make you wait too long," she said. "We were out in the backyard setting up the play set and didn't hear the bell, but I saw the shadow in the window and was hoping you were here."

"Yes, I rang the bell, but you must not have heard. Maybe your husband didn't hear it either," Ed said.

"My husband?" she replied. "It's just me and the kids here. We just moved in today."

"Well, the man in the window seemed like he saw me. He surely would have heard the bell, or maybe I was mistaken," Ed said.

"Yes, you must be," she replied. "The shadows from the street must have looked like something else."

"They must have," he replied. "I must apologize though. I am not the normal driver of this route. The old delivery guy typically drives this route. He told me he couldn't deliver here, so I took the delivery and got here as fast as I could. I hope it wasn't too long. I truly apologize," Ed said.

"No problem," she replied. "It wasn't too long. We were busy moving in anyway."

"Ok, it will be $11.35 then."

She handed him $15 and told him to keep the change. Ed thanked her for choosing the pizza place and he said next time he would get there quicker.

Ed walked back to his car and looked back three times to see if the shadow from the light off the street was still in the window. He felt very strange each time he looked back and did not see a shadow. No problem, he thought, and jumped in the car and pulled out onto the street, zipping away effortlessly in a flash.

The woman dropped the pizza on the table and went out the back door to the yard to finish setting up the play set. Half an hour went by before she remembered the pizza sitting on the table. It would surely be cold now, she thought.

"Kids, we need to go in and eat some dinner. I have pizza for us," she retorted.

"Yea!" they yelled and scrambled into the house and up to the table. She saw the pizza box and was queried. It was slightly opened and no one was in the house. She grabbed the pizza box and opened it all the way up. The kids were crowded around the table with paper plates and napkins in hand.

"Me first," the oldest said as she held her plate out.

"Ok, ok, I will get you some, but if it's too cold, we can heat it up on the microwave."

"Oh, it will be ok," the oldest replied.

9

The woman grabbed a piece out of the box and was amazed that it was still piping hot. That's not possible, she thought. The pizza was at least an hour and fifteen minutes old. There was no way it could be as hot as if it just came out of the oven.

"Come on, Mom!" the child cried. "I need some pizza! I am hungry!"

"Alright, here you go," she said as she handed out slices to each kid. They ate it up as fast as they could inhale it. It was the perfect pizza, hot and ready.

"Thanks, Mom," they all said as they left the table. They went to lay in the living room and watch television. She shirked her shoulders as she cleaned up and didn't think about the pizza again.

Chapter Two: Church

The blind men shout "Let the creatures out,
We'll show the unbelievers."
The napalm screams of human flames
Of a prime time Belsen feast, yeah!
As the reasons for the carnage cut their meat and lick
the gravy
We oil the jaws of the war machine and feed it with our
babies
The killer's breed or the demon's seed
The glamour, the fortune, the pain
Go to war again, blood is freedom's stain
Don't you pray for my soul anymore
Two minutes to midnight
The hands that threaten doom
Two minutes to midnight
To kill the unborn in the womb

-Iron Maiden, "Two Minutes to Midnight", 1984

The uneasy bewilderment of the moment felt surreal. The breeze wafted through the small, open stained glass windows. Philip didn't want to move or appear out of place as the service was going along normally. He peered over to his wife, Lydia, who was seated quietly. She appeared to be

11

strangely still with a glazed look of uneasiness. The atmosphere seemed unreal and each knew they had entered an altered dimension.

He held her hand tightly and she responded back. A voice could be heard suddenly from their side and they both looked over to a strange gentleman with a very familiar look. They seemed to know him, but the uneasy feeling grew. The man turned and looked to them quietly. He reached over to place his hand over her pregnant womb. Philip could hardly move and was helpless to respond. The gentleman spoke only these words.

"The boy will be disturbed and frustrated in this earthly place."

Then he was gone in the same instant he was there. They both were wondering how the man came and went so quickly when the bells began ringing. The bells normally rang during the Lord's Prayer. They both seemed to be drawn back to normal. The bells ended their ringing and they followed the end of the service in a strange silence.

The procession out of the church was just like every Sunday and they were the last to greet the pastor on the way out. The pastor had the look of relief as he was at the end of the last sermon of the day. He shook their hands and asked them how they had been. They both turned to look at each other and Philip quickly responded.

"Well, we did want to ask who the new gentleman was who sat next to us today."

The pastor looked puzzled and momentarily stumbled at a response. "Who?" he asked.

"The gentleman who sat right next to us and then left early," Lydia responded.

"I am not sure how to respond," the pastor said. "I was watching you during the service because I was concerned something was amiss. I felt I may be needed to come over there for a few minutes," the pastor said. "It was truly disconcerting as you had a blank stare on each of your faces, but I thought better. It was as if you both had a long night and were quite tired. I know how the church can be very consoling. I just took the time to watch over your way to make sure you two were alright today. I never saw anyone seated next to you though. You were all by yourselves throughout the entire service."

Philip and his wife thought they were sure something strange happened, but they were also sure the pastor would have seen it too. They left the church perplexed about the whole situation. The sun was shining brightly, which made the whole day seem to be something to be enjoyed.

The months passed quickly, and soon it was time for Philip and Lydia to welcome their new baby. Christian came into the world like any other child, right on time and healthy as could be. He had all his fingers and his toes, two ears, a mouth, and a nose just like his mother's. He was the apple of his father's eye and his mother's beaming glory. She held him tightly and marveled at the gift of life; a hundred years of life to look forward to. He would be the joy of their lives.

His dad smiled and beamed with light while his mom held him in her arms. Christian held an eerie glow about him. The nurses wondered at his aura, but they dared not try to put a finger on it, for the new parents were absolutely overjoyed at his birth. All things considered, the birth was momentous in of itself and Christian's parents were full of anticipation like each new parent enjoys.

Christian's infant years were absolutely normal and without regard for the multitude of time's treasured moments. He would eat well and rarely put up a fit. He seemed to his parents to be the most normal and easy child they could ever have.

It was always strange when they would bring him to see relatives for get-togethers and out to friend's houses where other children were. Everyone would always comment to Christian's parents about his air of confidence. It was completely tangible to the outsiders, but for Christian's parents he seemed completely normal. Christian had an uncanny knack for owning any room he was present in. He had an aura of completeness about him and seemed immune to anything or anyone around him. Christian was truly his own man, even at the youngest age.

The preschool years flew by fast for Christian. His mom would bring him to the early morning session so he could play and interact with the other kids, as he was their only child. His mom would see, once in a while, the difference in Christian compared to the other kids, but each time she would dismiss it.

The teachers would comment on how he would normally decide on a task to complete. Even if it was being used by another student, Christian would go over and stand near the other child playing for a few moments until the other child would surrender the learning task to him. It only took a few moments for the other child to want to relinquish the task, no matter what it was, or how enthralled the other child was with doing it. Christian was never mean or cruel about it. He was just dominating in an unreal way.

His mother desired for him to be special, just like every other parent. Each parent wants their child to be the special one. She knew it was part of being human and believing in her lineage that her child should be the one to lead the generations to come.

Christian, even in early interactions, was one to confidently set the tone and the mood. He wasn't bossy or pushy; he just commanded the tone and everyone conceded. He was the pinnacle of every room he went into, immediately and without question.

Chapter Three: Grade School

The year for first grade came quickly. His parents could hardly believe he was now a first grader. His mom dropped him off in the first grade room, staying long enough to give him a hug. She held her tears back seeing her little one on his own for the first time in her life. As she walked by the school windows, she couldn't hesitate to peer in and see how he was going to like the school year. She could see her normal view of Christian. He was confident and ready to tackle anything sent his way. He owned the room. She beamed with happiness and went home knowing he was alright.

It wasn't until later in the year when the parent teacher conferences were held, that Christian's parents were truly made aware of the things to come. His teacher hesitated repeatedly when going over his progress in first grade and they too felt uneasy about the meeting. It got so obvious that Christian's dad came out and asked the poignant question.

"What are you not telling us?" Philip asked.

The teacher looked into both of their eyes and started slowly, but surely.

"It's the demeanor of Christian, that I am sure you both know, that disturbs me so," she replied. "You see, he is a good learner and is really well behaved, but his demeanor is, well, quite frightening to me," she stuttered.

"His what?" Lydia replied, curiously, inquisitively, and unnervingly.

"Yes, his demeanor. I don't want you to think he is bad, it's just disturbing. I mean, he controls the room and all that he is around. I can't put my finger on it, but he is ingratiated in everything completely and there is nothing I, nor anyone else, can do. I have tried to separate myself out of this," she stuttered and then paused in deathly silence.

The teacher composed herself and continued, "Well, he has a spell, for lack of a better word, a controlling spell, over anywhere he goes. It is so disconcerting to me, that I have to unwind out of it for hours after school lets out each day. My husband cannot help me and he gets worried for me more and more. When the weekend comes around, I can get back to my normal, pleasant self and truly enjoy the fruitful nectar of life. On Monday, when I get back to school and Christian walks in, I fall back into a dark abyss. I fear his aura each moment, and my only solace are the religious classes each day."

Christian's parents sit stone quiet even after she stops talking.

"I don't know what to say," Lydia finally replied.

In utter silence they sat for what seemed like eternity. The door creaked and all three of them jumped nearly out of their seats. It was the principal poking her head around the door. Their collective sigh of relief was extremely noticeable. The principal even asked abruptly if they were alright. They all smiled and said yes, they were just finishing up. She told them the other parents are waiting and they assured her they were finished.

The principal left and closed the door. The teacher looked over to them and told them not to worry too much as it must be just something she was responsible for because Christian seemed to be a good kid and was doing quite well in all his studies. Christian's parents were inquisitively stunned, but could never bring themselves to believe their son was anything but a normally gifted child.

The years passed and Christian worked his way through grade school. He seemed to do just fine. He worked normally at all his studies and played well with others, but a different kind of play was his repertoire. He would always control and direct the entire scene. He was his own man and not in the leader sense. He commanded respect, and he demanded it in a quiet tone. No one dared question his resolve.

Chapter Four: Train - Transgression

His teenage years seemed to only change his demeanor, and not for the best. It was always normal for teenagers to ascend into their adult years with some form of struggle and Christian was no different.

His one nemesis was a tough kid from the other side of the tracks, though it should be said that Christian himself was from that same side of the tracks. It was not obvious to anyone but Christian and this instigator. He would feed off of Christian's demeanor and control the circumstances, but in a counter intuitive way. He would pester Christian in every way possible. Christian could handle anything except the downright resolve of his teenage nemesis.

It came down to one quite unimportant event. Christian was walking stride for stride with a group of teenage boys through the woods and along the trails they all knew too well. They had wandered these very trails so often they practically had footprints imbedded in the exact spot they each walked. Each boy knew their place in the pecking order of the trail walk and in their place in the hidden fort.

The days would go by in short order, and they ventured out into the woods to pass the time away either after school or during any break when the weather was well enough. It was this very day when his nemesis was at his worst when he bumped Christian off the trail while trying to be crass and walk out of line to a new spot in the group.

"Hey, move over Commander," the boy said as he pushed by. "You are moving like an iceberg and slow as molasses."

Every other boy could sense the extreme uneasiness of the walk. When they made it to the trail railroad crossing, each boy was on high alert, for today was the normal day for the train to make its run. Like clockwork it would come barreling around the bend when they crossed. They had been in this situation before when the train would seem to sneak up on them and they would jump as fast as they could off the tracks. Today was one of those days. They began to cross and there it was, the train.

It came up on them like it was coming out of a worm hole. They had little time to react, but Christian reacted extremely quickly. He cleared the rail and stood stoically on the edge of the gravel next to the weeds, silently and calmly. The other boys quickly made the move across, seemingly just in time. They all turned to see the train pass them in a reckless speed and that was when they saw the boy there. It was a moment of pure disbelief.

Christian looked on with a quiet, assured look. His nemesis was stuck. His foot was trapped in a place no one could imagine would hold him. He had no time to scream and they had no time to react. The train engineer was completely taken off guard and never hit the brakes until the boy's body was under the engine. The brakes squealed a deathly noise and they all stood there. They knew he was never to be heard from again. It was truly a tragedy no one is prepared to see, especially at that young age.

It was a long afternoon as they were all picked up by their parents after questioning. No one was to blame and each was left with a new understanding of life's denial of immortality. Christian was assuredly at peace and took everything in stride. His parents would console the other parents and the boy's parents in their loss.

The trail and the fort were never occupied again as the city put barriers up to make sure no other child could repeat the possibility of that walk again. During the investigation, the safety officials reviewed the location many times, but were never able to repeat the way the boy had become stuck on the rail. The accident was ruled a non-repeatable event, with no other precautions being initiated as no cause was ever found.

Part Two

Chapter Five: High School

Lines form on my face and hands
Lines form from the ups and downs
I'm in the middle without any plans
I'm a boy and I'm a man
I'm eighteen and I don't know what I want
Eighteen I just don't know what I want
Eighteen I gotta get away
I gotta get out of this place
I'll go runnin' in outer space oh yeah
I got a baby's brain and an old man's heart
Took eighteen years to get this far
Don't always know what I'm talkin' about
Feels like I'm livin' in the middle of doubt
'Cause I'm eighteen
I get confused every day
Eighteen, I just don't know what to say
Eighteen, I gotta get away

-Alice Cooper, "I'm Eighteen", 1970

    Time went by swiftly. They all grew up to go quickly onto high school. Christian was never any different. He would work through his freshman hazing, all the while doing well in class. He would be someone interesting enough to be around, but never someone who would be around for too long.

Each day, on his walk to school, he went past the church he belonged to. Christian always felt a sense of home as he walked toward it. He passed the well-worn sidewalk with grass. The weeds were growing steadfastly through the cracks. It was a sidewalk no handicapped person would dare to traverse. The bumps and cracks made it nearly impassable for even the sure footed pedestrian.

Christian knew this sidewalk well as he remembered the day it was poured brand new. He was there the day the hot sun shone down on the members of the church as they troweled the concrete to a perfectly smooth path for all to come to the church. He remembered the group asking if it was too hot and that it would surely crack as it dried too fast. They all debated whether to drape a cover over it and wet it down periodically to keep it moist and from drying too fast.

The church had been a wonder to envision. In his early years he would walk by and see it in all its glory, but lately he would walk by and see the church falling into disrepair. Each day was sadder and sadder for Christian to walk by, for he could remember when the church was a pillar of the community. Its minister was completely respected by everyone in the surrounding area. The people would come like clockwork to listen to his vision of each Bible lesson for the week. He seemed to know just how to interpret the story for the whole community to relate to.

Kurt was his name. Christian could sense the warmth and honor each and every time he could be at the service. Christian would walk by each day and reflect on the moments that led to this state of decline for the once predominant church. The church still held onto a regal past stature, in and of itself, but the ability for it to stay in its prominence was fading in the last few years. Kurt was the one focal point of life in the church. He was the life blood of the existence. He was the true, only reason for growth of the church. Christian could remember vividly the day when everything changed.

That Sunday was an early summer service. Though the church was never in need of parishioners, typically it was the summer months when the church was less filled and especially since the pastor was on vacation. It was seemingly quieter then he could remember. Little did anyone know, except Christian, who knew inside before anything was said, that it would be a day that would be a defining moment in all their lives.

The church organ played the opening song while deacons rang the bells to invite the congregation to the service. The visiting pastor stepped up to the front of the church sanctuary, but today he stepped forward past the first pews, and momentarily stood quietly. The sense of something out of place was palpable. Each member knew the words that would come out of his mouth would be grave. Christian knew exactly what was about to be said. Then the pastor spoke.

"Members, I have something truly disconcerting to tell you today. It is with heavy heart I need to tell you, but with some solace I can tell you here in this place of warm security. We have lost someone, your rock and pillar of this church. It is with great sadness I must tell you, Pastor Kurt was lost at sea last night. His boat was found intact and floating, but it appears he was lost overboard in an unexplained incident. He was sailing off the Michigan coast in the middle of

Lake Michigan with we believe to be normal weather. I know this is something he has done for years and he was along the very route he normally takes. We have no information on his disappearance. We held out hope to maybe find him when the dawn broke. There was no such luck. Kurt was an avid boater and an experienced scuba diver. He was the pillar of all he came in contact with and will be sadly missed."

The congregation was silently still. A sound was nowhere to be heard. The fans that kept the air flowing spun eerily silent. It was at that very moment a butterfly flew over to the front of the church. It landed majestically on the baptismal font. Each person in the sanctuary was mesmerized. They watched intently as the butterfly slowly waved its wings and then flew out as miraculously as it flew in. The moment lasted for an eternity.

Christian sat inquisitively as the pastor returned to his chair. The organ began to play softly and longingly. The sun shone through the stained glass windows all through the service as if it was beamed in. Christian could sense a defining moment in time. It was the very moment he realized his need for the connection to the church.

He knew it would never be the same and now he was on his own of sorts. He had the tools and the knowledge to make a go of it for the rest of his life. His parents sat stunned throughout the service, just as the other parishioners did.

Chapter Six: Pastor - Compassion

A gathering of angels
Appeared above my head
They sang to me this song of hope
And this is what they said
They said come sail away, come sail away
Come sail away with me
Come sail away, come sail away
Come sail away with me
I thought that they were angels
But to my surprise
They climbed aboard their starship
And headed for the skies

-Styx, "Come Sail Away", 1977

Christian stood outside that day, peering at the dilapidated building and wondering how it all came to be and why. Was it the true reason, as the pastor said that day, that there was a greater need for Pastor Kurt to be in heaven? Was it a mission he had, to help others in another life? Christian could only hope it was all true. It was the only plausible explanation that could help him move forward in life, knowing there would be a time he was needed somewhere other than in this life, in this body. The church was magnificent to Christian, even in its present condition. His memories would always be of the life filled house.

He remembered the stories truly and succinctly until this day. The pastor was an avid fisherman. His sailing skills were second to none. He would fish each moment he had to himself. There were times some parishioners would go out with him or sit on the docks casting their poles to catch a fish. Maybe they were fishing for something other than fish though. Maybe it was the time needed to contemplate life with a caring person. Kurt would always be that person.

He surely would have been fishing by himself, collecting his thoughts, but he never once turned down a request for others to join him. Kurt was the epitome of a pastor. He was truly devoted to helping others through challenging times. He shared the best of times in all their glory. He never dared to let on that he had such a human side. There were times he would assuredly like to be alone in his solace to fish on the docks, pondering the gift of life. He thought about all that life had to give to everyone in their journey through time. Each person had a short time to be on this earth. It should be savored in its entirety. Kurt was one to understand the precious gift of life in each miniscule moment.

It was one of the many sailing trips he took north through Lake Michigan. He would be at one with the human and conscience sides of being Kurt. The sailing on the wide open waters of Lake Michigan helped him become one with all life had given him. He understood and was ready to share what was coming for him in the future. He looked forward to a clear, undisturbed journey alone with his thoughts. His sail boat was not the largest vessel, but was always perfectly maintained. The sail boat he named *Compassion*, truly was his place of peace. He kept her up to date as well as he could on a pastor's salary. She was his pride and joy.

His moments out on Lake Michigan let him pretend he was out on an ocean voyage. He dreamed he was circling the globe, just he and his boat, one with nature. It was a true partnership, helping each other in times of pleasant weather or in times of violent storms. They were out there by themselves, fending as best they could. Their lives were in each other's hands completely. He had the strongest faith in her to carry him home, no matter how the events made it seem impossible.

Lake Michigan afforded him this small bit of adventure, as he could sail out far enough to lose sight of land. This was where he could keep his fantasy of ocean voyages alive. He let his long hair down, twisting in the wind, as the sound of the sails ruffled taut in the wind. It wafted him and his boat out into the wide open water. Kurt was at home, in every sense of the word, on the vast open waters of Lake Michigan. Nary a soul knew how far he traveled on his adventures. He could have gone only out to open waters and drifted around or he could have traveled far up north, utilizing the strong winds to make his journey quick. His mid-week getaways were his respite from the daily activities.

Christian could only wonder what happened that fateful day, for no one has ever had a clue of the events that unfolded. They only had clues to Kurt's disappearance. Kurt had set sail early on a Tuesday morning with all his gear in tow. His sail boat was prepped for a long two days on the water. He had packed all he needed to sail through the day, spend the night on the water, then sail the next day. He would dock back in the harbor.

The church was caught up on all its activities. The office was tidied up. The visits to the hospital and nursing homes were all taken care of. Kurt must have left that day with a smile on his face. The wind was at his back, with the warm jet stream coming directly out of the southwest. He surely had his best time setting the sail and manning the ropes to keep her drifting north at a happy clip.

He could have taken her way north the first day. He could have gone past the point of turning east, and went to St. Joseph, Michigan, to stop for a restful lunch. His trip must have been picture perfect, sailing effortlessly, and cutting through the water quietly. His trip was one of true spiritual enlightenment. Maybe he had wandered into a unique moment in time in what some have come to call the Lake Michigan Triangle.

Christian had heard of some stories about it. The triangle stretched from Ludington to Benton Harbor, Michigan and to Manitowoc, Wisconsin. Kurt truly would have been squarely in the middle of it later that day, Christian thought.

From missing boats, to missing planes, to missing people, the stories varied widely with each rendition Christian heard. Kurt would have been right there, he thought.

He must have seen the heart of the triangle. Maybe it was a vortex. Maybe a quick squall came out of nowhere. Some stories had talked about a portal or worm hole, like the back holes in space. Some people have seen mysterious craft coming in and out of the water. It could be a hidden gate to another time or place. Kurt must have seen this. Maybe his treasured craft journeyed into the portal to drift to another time and place.

This was the best sort of ending Christian could hang on to. It was the only plausible ending which left the hope open for his safe return. If he did not return to his Christian life, then maybe Kurt could return in some future time, when the church could again be revived to its former glory. Christian could always hold out hope.

The congregation dwindled over the years. It was not long before the church could not sustain it existence and it closed for good. Christian's parents were so distraught they could not find the motivation to attend any other church. They had lost their way in the faith. Christian had lost a basic piece of a foundation he so needed.

As each day passed, Christian's faith wandered. It faded into a wash of normal everyday life. Like a plant not tended to, it withered away, and was seemingly dead.

Chapter Seven: Crosley

High school went by in a flash. Christian's dad, Philip, worked hard each day to support the family. Christian looked up to his dad for being so faithful and providing for them. He would someday hope to be half the man his dad was. It was not long until Christian was graduating as a senior. His grades were good and his outlook on life seemed to be picking up.

The day was in early June and Christian was hoping to enjoy a little summer time off with his friends. He woke up normally mid-morning to get something to snack on. As he sat at the table eating his breakfast obliviously, he heard the front door open and wondered who it could be. His dad was at work and everyone else was in the living room. Christian shot up out of his chair and ran to the door only to find it was his dad, who was beaming ear to ear.

Christian stopped suddenly in front of him and smiled quickly as he saw his dad's hand holding a set of keys. They looked new and gleaming as if they were just cut. A cheap, tacky key ring held exactly what Christian knew them to be for, a new car. His dad smiled and held out his hand to give him the keys.

"These are for you. This car is yours," his dad said proudly, giving the keys to his son.

"What?" Christian said startled. "For me?" he said inquisitively.

"Yes, for you. I was hoping it would be a surprise and I can see it was," he smiled.

"Oh, thanks Dad! You are the best!"

Christian grabbed the keys and ran out the door. In his peripheral vision he could see his mom come out of the living room as he shot out of the front door. Christian wasted no time going to see the car. It was small and a brand new shade of red. His friends had cars, but no one had a new one. It was not a high end car, but it was new.

The car gleamed with a shine only a new car that was freshly cleaned could do in the mid-morning sun. Christian walked around it to take in all its glory. His dad had made his way outside by that time.

"So, what do you think?" Philip asked.

"Oh, Dad, it's great!"

"Yes, and it's new, too. I thought you would like it," he replied. "It's small, but it's a new Crosley. I thought you would like the sporty red, so it took a few extra days to get it. I was sure you wouldn't mind. It's your graduation present."

"Wow! Thanks Dad, you're the best. Mom too," Christian said.

His mom, Lydia, beamed back, for she felt a truly emotional sense of relief. Christian was clearly on his way to being a vital part of society where he would contribute positively.

"It really is different, isn't it?" Christian asked.

"Yes, it's a small car with good gas mileage. It is really unique. It has a different kind of metal engine," Philip said.

"What?" Christian said and turned immediately around.

"Yes, let me show you," his dad said as he opened the hood. "See, it's not cast, it is made out of metal. Some call it a tin engine. It really is a marvel and helps keep the cost down."

"Oh cool, and that means I get a new car."

"You are right, that means you get a new car."

"Thanks so much, Dad," Christian said again.

His dad could not remember the last time he saw Christian in such an uplifting spirit, but this surely was one of those times. Christian climbed into the front seat of the car. He assumed a comfortable driving position. He could smell the new smell of the car filling the air. It was the smell of new materials. It had an aroma of overtones of the multitude of glues used in all the materials assembled in the car.

He deftly adjusted the seat lever to give him the most commanding seating position. He wanted to look cool behind the wheel. He always made fun of his friend who drove around in a laid back slant, so that just wasn't his style. He could easily reach all the knobs and levers from his newly adjusted seat. He knew it would work well for him to drive around in this car.

The radio was just in the perfect location for him to tune different stations on the go. He really enjoyed listening to the radio as much and anywhere he could. Now he could tune to different stations as he drove along. The heating and vent levers where in a quick reach location just below the radio knobs. He slid them back and forth to get a feel of the friction at each setting. The hot and cold temperature lever would do well in the colder months. He knew the cold side of the lever really just meant grabbing air from the outside. Air from the outside was only as good as the outside temperature. In mid-August it would surely be only as cool as the speed he was driving.

He brushed his hand across the dashboard to recognize he would take of his new car. The radio station he first picked belted out a recent hit of love lost. He knew it well. He took a moment to listen to parts of it before he turned the key to start the engine. He then fired up the car and swiftly drove off to his friend's house. They surely would want to go for a ride and maybe an adventure.

Philip gave his wife a hug. Since he had the day off now, he moved the family car into the garage to do some maintenance on it before he had to go back to work.

Christian enjoyed the car immensely all summer, even though some quirks showed up. He got frustrated sometimes, but he always found a way to go about fixing it and going out with his friends. The car ended up to be a poor quality car. Christian's dad was not a mechanic, but he was mechanically gifted and always found a way to keep the little car going. Christian would get so frustrated each time the tin engine in the car would act up.

The end of the summer came quickly and his friends seemed to be moving on to jobs or college. It was a quiet, late summer day and the dew was beginning to form on the grass at night. One morning his dad came into the kitchen to eat breakfast before going to work. Christian was having his normal, nothing special breakfast. His dad sat down, took a few bites, and started the conversation.

"So, what are you up to now?" his dad asked.

Christian looked over and shrugged his shoulders. "Not much," he said.

"How about getting a job?"

"Well, that might be ok," Christian replied.

"How about if you had a good job?" his dad kept on.

Christian perked up and looked at his dad. "Like what?" he asked.

"I have a friend in the mills who said they are looking for a few good new recruits if you are interested. You would be a beginning union trainee, but it could lead to a good, full time, well-paying job," his dad said and smiled.

Christian knew all too well it was a great job opening. He knew some of his older friends worked at the mills and made a very good living. He knew from being at their houses that they were well paid. A couple of his friends were only two years out of high school and they had their own houses. He always thought it was really neat that they had their own place and he could hang out with them. They were young and had life by the horns.

"Well, what do you think?" his dad asked.

"That would be great!" Christian beamed.

"Ok then, I will write down the address and you can go there today to apply."

Philip got up from eating, wrote down the address on the memo paper, and made his way out of the kitchen.

"Hey!" Christian shouted out.

"Yes, Son?"

"Thanks, Dad! You are the best!"

His dad came back into the room and gave him a hug as if to say he would do anything for his son. That moment was one of the few times in life when his dad could remember being so close to Christian.

Christian applied and got the job at the mills. It was a whirlwind time each day he went to work. The job paid well. In no time, Christian was a regular worker, making his shift, and getting his job done. He went out with his friends every weekend to many places to have fun, meet others, and hopefully to meet girls. The weekends went by so fast and he had his own small apartment to live in.

Chapter Eight: Love

The weeks flew by and soon each of his friends was meeting someone special. Christian met a special girl who seemed to know just how to understand him and his quirks. She even understood his disturbed side, the side he tried so hard to hide so to not be a burden on the group and spoil the evening. She was his steadfast supporter. Each time he would fall into the downers, she would be right by his side. After many months of hanging out and a few weddings of his friends, Christian knew she was the one.

One gloriously warm Saturday in September, he was with her parked in the parking lot overlooking the lake and the sand dunes. They had stopped at the malt shop to get something to eat and drink. He had a milkshake and she had an ice cream cone as they sat watching the sun getting ready to set over the lake. Christian had known for weeks this moment was for them. He put his milkshake down to get out of the car.

"Why don't we sit outside? It's nice out," he said.

"Ok," she replied as she got out of the car.

Christian made his way around the car to quickly and adeptly get down on one knee. She knew instantly.

"Oh, Christian," she said.

"Yes, I have this for you and one big question," he said as he kneeled down. "Will you marry me?" he asked.

She grabbed him up and held him tight. "Yes, I will, thank you so much. I love you," she said, as they embraced in the setting sunlight.

The wedding was a warm and thoughtful event. Christian's parents were filled with happiness, as they could sense Christian's new outlook on life. The gifts from the wedding helped them put a down payment on a new house on the south side of town. It was in a new subdivision in the ever expanding town. They were so happy to be moving into a new house and beginning a life together with their friends and raising a family.

Chapter Nine: Angel

The months passed ever so quickly. The very special days of quiet, peaceful enjoyment sitting in the backyard and enjoying the cool evening air seemed strangely unique today. Christian knew in all his being that something was quite different and had been quite different for days now or even weeks. He would taste the difference in the home cooked dinners and the aura of magic around the house. He was not one to admit it, but he knew that she knew. Nevertheless, it was that cool evening she spoke.

"Christian?"

"Yes, dear?" he replied.

"We need to get one of the bedrooms in order in the next few weeks."

"Ok," he replied in a pacifying way. He knew what was next.

"You know, ready as in a place for the baby to sleep," she said.

Christian peered over by simply turning his head but not his whole body and smiled brightly. "That would be wonderful," he said. She smiled back and reached out to hold his hand for the moment they would cherish forever.

"With this baby coming, we need to make plans as a family," he said.

"Yes, we need to plan our future for the coming years, the house, the finances, and all."

"Oh, yes," he replied. "We can do that." Christian turned his head back to lean on the tall chair and peered to the sky. He was inevitably filled with worry. Would the baby be like him and be an uneasy, troubled, and frustrated person or would the baby be spared and follow in his loving wife's angelic ways? He could only hope.

The months passed in their ever increasing pace now that the baby was coming. It felt like it was only yesterday they were making plans for the baby and then the baby was born. It was a beautiful girl, healthy and well with all her faculties. When she breathed her first breath, Christian knew she was not like him in anyway and her name appeared to him instantly. He held her, smiled, and looked into her glowing face.

"Aricka," he said. "Welcome to the world. We are so happy to meet you."

His wife smiled, even through the weary physical exhaustion.

"Aricka. That is a pretty name," his wife said.

"Yes, it came to me like a vision. She is my angel, my very own angel on earth," he said.

Each day passed with love and adoration for his daughter. She truly was the angel of his life. Christian spent each moment home from work with her. He would talk all day about her at work, his special angel all his coworkers knew her to be. They could see she brought out the best in him; a side they never knew existed. His days were a treasure to live with his little angel in his life.

A couple of years went by and they had a son also. He was a normal child and he made Christian happy too, but he was smitten by his first born daughter. He worked hard picking up any shift he could get, so he could bring some more money home for his family. They lived well and only needed more a few times of the year. Christian would always provide and find a way, with his wife's help, to make it all work out.

He would lean on his dad often, to make sure his vehicles worked, as his luck with anything automobile related would never work out. He was the most frustrated with the automobiles he had. He seemed to be the unluckiest guy ever, from flat tires to bad fuel to defective mechanicals. He even once bought a new battery in the dead of winter to replace the old one. Of course it was not truly worn out; it just decided to quit working. When he was installing it, it sparked and he watched it completely melt into oblivion. Sure enough, he phoned his dad for help and sure enough his dad was on the spot to get it going. If it wasn't for his dad, who knows how many times he would not have made it to work.

Part Three

Chapter Ten: Father

Risk my soul, test my life
For my bread
Spend my time lost in space
Am I dead?
Let the river flow
Through my callused hands
And take me from my own
The eyes of the damned
It makes my stomach turn
And it tears my flesh from the bone
How we turn a dream to stone
And we all die young
Yeah we all die young

-Steel Dragon, "We All Die Young", 2001

  Christian worked hard, but he had a truly
dark side his family nearly never saw. He was a
true steelworker in the sense he would work the
long, hard, hot shifts and then stop at the local bar
to settle his mind and body in the bottom of
several glasses of alcohol. It was his respite for the
drudgery he endured each day. He would sit at the
bar and ponder his troubles and frustration in all

he did. It was only in his moments of thinking of his blessed family that would bring him respite.

It was a warm, late summer night. The wind wafting through the leaves in the trees that lined the street calmed Christian down. He was walking along the main street to get to his parked car after a long day of working far too hard.

It was the momentary glimpse that drew him to the store front window. A picture perfect butterfly necklace sat perched atop the tall display. It struck him with a great sense of serenity. He could picture his own daughter wearing it when she got big enough. It symbolized everything he treasured about Aricka. She was his angel, his guiding light, his perfect butterfly.

Christian was never one to even contemplate about buying jewelry, but this beautiful pink butterfly necklace commanded him to change his ways. He was somehow being summoned into the store to purchase the pink butterfly pendant.

Just as he was around his daughter Aricka, he was powerless to avoid getting this for her. A side of him struggled to go into the store, saying it's late, the store is not even open, so you can't buy it. The other helpless compassionate side drove him to walk up the store front to check the door to see if it was open.

Pulling on the handle, it opened easily. The jewelry store beckoned him to come in. A frail older lady came out from behind the counter, seemingly startled to see someone in the store.

"Oh, dear," she said. "I thought I had locked that. See, we closed a little while ago."

"I'm sorry," he said, "but I was mesmerized by the butterfly necklace in the window. I just had to have it."

"Oh, dear, you have a kind eye. It just came in yesterday. I just put it up in the display case a few minutes ago. I was hoping it would draw some attention tomorrow when we opened for the weekend, but I see it worked all too well," she said. "Here you are."

"Thank you," he replied. "I am not sure how much it is, but please wrap it up in a nice jewelry box. It's for my infant daughter when she gets older."

"Well, that sounds swell," she said. "I will put it in a long lasting jewelry box so when you are ready to give it to her, she will be very happy. It will make a great gift. This very necklace came from an importer out east. It was the only one of its kind in the lot of jewelry. My buyer was traveling out east when he came across this gifted jeweler with some rare items. This one was very special to him, as he purchased the whole lot."

She carefully handled the necklace from the display case. She set it in a small, velvet jewelry case. The lid snapped tightly shut. She wrapped it in a pretty paisley blue and red paper. A silk pink bow tie wrapped around the case to hold it all together.

"Thank you," she said, as she handed it to Christian.

He was dumbfounded in holding the small bag with the necklace in it. Carefully, he placed the bag in the passenger seat as he drove home for the evening.

Few to none ever saw this side of Christian. Usually, he did his best to maintain a tough exterior. If there ever was a fight or heated scuffle, he would step right up to shut it down. He would always try to help the little guy in the battle. More often than not, he would end up the loser in the end, bruised, battered, and sore all the way home. It never distracted him from work though, and each day the daily tale was true to form. Work hard each day, toil in the heat of the molten steel ladle, just to make it to the bar for the nectar of relief in the bottom of a glass of alcohol.

Everyone left him alone at work and at the bar, as it seemed he preferred that. He would grunt and snarl at anyone around him each moment, but would get the task done one way or another. His work ethic was never questioned, but his demeanor was something not to be crossways with.

The scuffles he entered into, whether of his own or the ones that found him, would end, but would not be final. After each scuffle, the one who deserved retribution found a way to come to unexpected tough times. It was normal for anyone that seemed to deserve some retribution to get it after being involved in a scuffle where Christian was involved. From a car accident, to a choking, or even an unknown sickness, the foes of Christian all paid dearly.

There was one blatant characteristic of Christian's that everyone knew too well. No one ever discussed it or even attempted to bring it up. Somehow, some way, Christian had an utter disdain for ethnic people. He was a well-known unadulterated bigot. His wife would go out of her way to make sure the circumstances never came up where he would be around ethnic people. The colored people would send him into orbit of which it would take hours for him to calm down. At work it was known by supervisors to keep him away from any ethnic people. They knew he would be worthless if he was set off. He worked so well and strong they never wanted him to be set off.

A day off, working outside the house, for Christian was normally pleasurable, unless someone of color would walk by. It set him off immediately, and he yelled at them and chased them down the street, sometimes like a madman out of his mind. His daughter, Aricka, would grow up knowing her dad could easily be set off. There were days she would ride up and down the block to make sure no one came down the street to set him off.

She learned early, even on her first tricycle that he helped her glide down the sidewalk along the block. As she grew and graduated to a two wheeled bicycle, it just afforded her the ability to get to each side of the block quicker to check for people coming down the street. She knew it would only set her dad off. She was the self-proclaimed sentry to make sure his outdoor time was as pleasurable as it could be. Her dad worked very hard at work, so she wanted him to have the most relaxing time at home when he was away from work.

Over the years, she just learned to accept him and love him for who he was, her father.

Chapter Eleven: Steel - Judgement

It was a hot as the blazes Tuesday afternoon. Christian had been working a long shift. The last ladle of molten iron was coming out of the furnace and true to form Christian was adeptly handling the maneuvering. It was a tricky slide out of the furnace and a shift in direction from the rail. It was the most dangerous job in the mill, but stubborn Christian made a point to be the one to do it each day. Each mill worker knew the dangers and always hoped Christian would show for work. There were no way any of them dared to volunteer for the job. The heat from the cauldron of steel was unbearable, even to the heartiest of souls, except for Christian.

There he was, on top of the ladle, and sometimes near the edge of its hot rim, just soaking up the heat. It was as if he was born to handle any amount of heat that you could throw at him. It was a normal operation for the ladle to move out and then shift directions for the pouring line.

Christian was there, right on top, when the ladle moved to the shift point. It stuck momentarily at the direction rail change. The motors ground and made a screeching sound as the ladle stuck steadfastly in its positon. On the transition point, Christian motioned for the rail operator to back it off a bit and then run it forward hard. The motors groaned to a stop, as it went in the opposite direction, to send the ladle back a few feet. Christian whirled his hands to motion the rail operator to go full speed. It was a very dangerous move, but one Christian had practiced many times before. The operator went full speed ahead. The motors moaned the hurt squeal of pushing them to their limits. A horrendous thud rang though out the plant. Everyone stopped working to find out the reason.

Christian stood there, as frustrated as he had ever been. The rail operator shrugged his shoulders, so Christian could see he gave it all the motors had. In a fit of complete rage and frustration, Christian pounded his fist wildly on the chain holding the ladle.

By now, more people had gathered around the sight. Most knew they would witness yet another of Christian's signature moves, one very few could ever witness. Christian waved his arms to the operator to back it up once again and then full speed ahead as quickly as the motors would allow.

The motors whirred again in reverse and then moved abruptly forward, jolting the ladle fully forward and ahead. Christian gripped the chain tight as the ladle made it to the switch point and then stopped hard with the loudest bang anyone had ever heard. He was even more infuriated and he jumped up and down. The rail operator thought he even saw Christian giving the ladle the one finger salute. The operator chuckled a bit and looked over to the growing crowd on the plant floor.

A body curdling scream rang out and the rail crane operator looked over just in time to catch a glimpse of Christian's body sinking into the molten steel cauldron. He knew exactly what happened. The ladle was now past the switch and the jolt of movement caught Christian off balance and he fell in.

There was no choice in that scenario for the ladle guy. He would either fall in the molten steel or fall off and to the concrete plant floor. The operator had seen it many times in his career and knew it was sad, but it was better to fall into the steel, instead of suffering a long cruel death by falling to the concrete floor below.

A hush set over the crowd. They knew completely what had just happened. The workers all removed their hard hats in honor of the fallen. The safety sirens went off in full roar. A complete shutdown was in effect.

It was only a few moments until the emergency evaluation team showed up.

"Here come the big guys," the operator shouted below to the astonished workers. "See there are Durapo and Callahan. When they come out, we are all going to pay attention, boys!" he yelled.

Durapo and Callahan looked up with a stern look on their faces. It was the "you all know better" sort of look. They were responsible for all the safety training. They were responsible for each worker staying cognizant of what they were doing. They knew this was not going to be fun in anyway. Every time something safety oriented happened, they would have to explain, report, and retrain everyone involved. The look they gave the operator said all that, in no uncertain terms. The operator looked back at them in a sheepish frown. He knew too this was the start of a long road back to trusting the workers to work safe. They all knew today was a day someone paid the ultimate price and was not going home.

Each worker knew when they walked through, that it was a very, very, bad day. It was a bad time. The team hustled through the plant. They were made up of fully suited emergency crew guys. Then came a team of emergency medical technicians. They were followed closely by a couple of business suited individuals, who were trailed only by the worker representatives. The union representatives were out of their lair.

They walked at a pace nearing a jog. They went deliberately through the machines. As they passed, each worker knew, like an innate sense, that something was horribly wrong, but they dared not leave their work post. The suits were always in a lather. They looked completely clueless compared to the other team members, who were clearly in their element. They knew exactly how to react. They went about their duties with compassion and steadfastness. The business suits just seemed to get in the way.

The crane operator, now standing on the safety platform, looked down to see the team. "EET," he said quietly, but the team surely heard it. They looked up, then wildly motioned to him to get the ladle moved. The emergency medical technician needed to get the operator on the radio. He brought his own radio to his ear while pointing to the operator, motioning for him to do the same. The crane operator knew what he meant. He hustled back to the crane cab to get his portable radio. It crackled immediately, loudly, and with force.

"Get that ladle over on the rail!" the speaker screamed. "Right now!"

The crane operator moved over to the safety platform, shrugged his shoulders, then pushed the talk button. "That's what we were trying to do! It's locked up!" he shouted into the mic.

"Well, get it moved now!" they returned.

He shrugged his shoulders again as he reached for the hydraulic lever. "Don't they think I would have moved it already?" he mumbled.

"What a bunch of idiots," he said. He pulled the lever anyway, knowing it would never move.

It wasn't but a split second later that he hit the lever to make it glide onto the rail precisely into place. Stunned, he flipped the transfer switch to change the route of the ladle to the side run for a set aside. "Hmm," he thought, as he sat there completely stunned. He did not expect that, so he let off the transfer lever. The engine purred to a stop. Quietly the ladle stopped on the track. It was perched cleanly in a place it seemed destined to sit.

In sheer moments, the EET crew was on the safety platform looking over the ladle rim. Sure enough, the boiling steel maintained a steady rhythm of bubbles, with each one cresting after the other. Christian was nowhere to be seen. There was not a speck of him or anything about him left. Even a possible footprint was not to be seen.

It took the crew a couple of hours to review the evidence. Each member went about their task like clockwork. First, the medical crew cleared all possible chances of finding any part of Christian. Then they left. The government regulators clamored around, looking at every inch of the crane and the rails. The business suits stood like mannequins next to the safety rails. They never budged a speck. The worker representative interviewed the crane operator, along with the best well-dressed suit, who must have been the on-call corporate lawyer. The government rep stood within ear shot to write down everything he heard. It went on for about two hours.

As each one finished up their standard protocol duties, they left. After all was said and done, the ladle sat ready to move over back to the main rail. With nothing left to decide, the foreman signaled the crane operator to transition the ladle back into the line. He motioned the sign of the cross across his chest. The operator worked the levers to help it gain momentum back to the production rail. The ladle smoothly transitioned to the production rail.

"Well, I'll be," the operator said out loud. He was dumbfounded. There was no way that did that just now, he thought. After all that, it just swiftly moved along like it was meant to be, like a hot knife going through butter. He raised his eyebrows in the quirky fashion he had been known for, and let the ladle run down the rail out of his sight. He pondered all the rest of the shift, all the way home, and all through the night what had just happened. It brought new meaning to his life for a small period of time, just like each major accident he had seen.

Chapter Twelve: Ingot - Mercy

The ladle went right through production, ending up on the steel ingot line. That line was set up for all steel transfers to each product ordered from the mill. The orders were normal that day. Each ingot was tagged and sent along the line to transfer to its next operation. The ingot from the mid-level of the now infamous ladle was stamped and tagged like all the others. It was tagged as a mid-level grade steel to be sent to various production orders, like a fence operation, a cannery, or even an appliance factory stamping order. The technician hooked the paperwork on it, but he knew where it came from, so he momentarily removed his hard hat and silently had a conversation with a higher power.

"Come on, down there, we need to get these out," his down line production worker called out. The technician looked up, put his hat on, and selected the button to move the ingot on. It arrived at the lift point to be set upon the order truck. Just as it was set to be lifted onto the next truck, the driver tapped the shoulder of the operator.

"Hey, I am short one here," he said holding out his paper work. "This says I need seven, but you only loaded six. What is up? You trying to get me in trouble? You know the production lines are roaring and I'm the low guy on the totem pole for the third major auto manufacturer in America. I need the other steel!"

"Yes, yes, I know, you always have to tell me each time. You know I would never let you get less than you ordered," the operator replied and winked back at him. "But you sure sing a different tune when your orders are low and you ask me to specifically short you sometimes."

"I know, and I really appreciate you doing me a swell one those times, but today I need the whole order."

"Ok, ok, I can give you this one," he said as he pulled the order from off the clamp and moved it to the next one. "You can have this one. It should do you wonders," he winked.

The driver was clueless, but he didn't care. He was happy to have the full load. It only took a few moments to load it on the trailer bed. He strapped it down and roared his older truck to life.

The ingot was on its way to a life it was never intended to have, but was it really intended to be on that path in the first place?

The old semi loaded with ingots traveled out of the mill yard and rolled down the interstate flawlessly. Traffic was light, but there was a completely obnoxious driver tailgating the semi for miles. The driver kept looking back and even motioned him to pass and go around. His semi was at full tilt. He had no more to give to get going at a faster speed. The tailgater kept on. It seemed he was destined to be a real pain in the caboose. The driver found a way to ignore the tailgater for miles. The road was straight without any bumps. He ran his semi true to the lanes with no worries.

The driver heard a loud crash and the semi jerked violently. "What the heck?" he said quickly. "What was that?" he said as he let off the gas. He put the truck in neutral and applied the brakes. The truck stopped easily over a short distance. He peered into his rearview mirror to see a mess behind him. "Oh, no," he said.

The mess was one of his ingots square on top of the tailgater's hood. The car looked like a flattened piece of tin foil all the way up to the dashboard. After running back to the car, he could see the driver, who was white as a ghost and clinging tightly to his steering wheel. He looked paralyzed.

"Are you alright?" he asked. "Hey, you are you all right?" he repeated.

The driver moved his eyes and only his eyes to look over to him. "What?" he asked.

"Are you alright there?"

"Yes, I think so."

"What happened?" the semi driver asked.

"I don't know," the tailgater said. "All I know is this steel brick jumped right off your bed and smack onto the top of my hood. I can still see the jump now. It actually jumped off the bed and like in slow motion it landed perfectly onto my car hood. I could swear it had perfect trajectory to land on my hood. I thought for sure I would be dead."

"Well, you are really lucky. These ingots, oh sorry, steel bricks, play no favorites when they let loose. You are one in a million here. At that speed and that distance behind me it should have landed right on your head. I have never seen this happen like this before."

It took hours for the tow truck drivers and a loader to get the ingot off the hood of the car and back on the truck trailer.

The dawn of a new day rose above the horizon as the semi driver pulled into the yard behind the industrial building. He turned his truck around and backed slowly to the loading dock.

"I heard you had a wild delivery ride," the dock operator quipped.

"Yes, you would not believe it," he replied. "One in a million, one in a million. It's this ingot here. This one is really strange."

"Oh, yea, you and your strange, man you always get me going," the dock guy said. "I will take care of your strange then," he chimed.

"No, you will see this one is really different."

The dock guy hopped onto the forklift. It whirred to life and he slipped the forks under the

79

load. The weight of the steel made the forklift groan, but it lifted the ingot up mightily. He drove it to the line for reduction down rolling. The ingot slipped quietly into the long hot oven and become white hot. It was a hot far hotter than the usual red hot. It was hot enough to mold any grade of steel into a roll for stamping. Out of the oven end, the wide, finely measured steel sheet flowed. It fed into a roller to be wound up for inventory. The quality control and strength technician snipped a small square out for review and put it into a test box with a check sheet for the date and time operator.

The steel was wound tightly and perfectly into shape to be bound for setting off to its next step. The outside crane operator hooked the chains through the coil and lifted it to its inventory line in the back row, three over from the aisle. A chalk mark on its outside face marked its number, date, and length. It sat waiting for its review and release.

Chapter Thirteen: Testing

The technician took all his samples on his cart. He wheeled them down the white colored halls and turned into the lab. All the samples were placed on the lab table in a line, ready for testing. He had been through this so many times he could do this in his sleep. Each sample would go through each testing station. He tested them in order of removal to find that each one, of course, passed the qualities they were ordered for.

He had gotten blasé in his testing as it had been a full three times that a sample hadn't passed a test, but even then they ordered him to send them out anyway. He had long ago lost his desire to catch a problem and have it actually mean something, but today a sample from one roll was intriguing him. It was running through the tests with high flying results. Each test it exceeded the parameters far and above anything he had ever seen.

The destructive temperature tests were his first clue. It held out to the 99th percentile, an amazing feat he had only heard of, but never seen. After thousands of tests, this sample passed with amazing results. He kept testing all the other samples for the day, as each one came back with normal results.

A couple of times, while doing some of the other samples, he could swear he could catch a glimpse of the remarkable test sample moving or maybe even changing. He had an eerie feeling it was shape shifting somehow. It seemed to be returning to its original size and shape. It was really late and he figured he was just overly fatigued.

The other tests went exactly the same, with each sample performing within tolerances except for the one unique sample. It always out-performed the others by a wide margin. It was not just at the edge of the range limit, but way above it.

The last test was his favorite, the destructive test. This was where the rubber hit the road. He would test the sample until it split in two. It was a true, results orientated test. It was complete destruction of the material down to the molecular level. It was always the most fun. When the sample got to the point of release, the sound was deafening as it snapped right in two.

He knew exactly which one he wanted to do, but he knew he had to wait until the end and do that one last. He had a suspicion it might even break the machine before it let go. He wanted to see, but he had to wait until the end, so he could call it a night and go home. Breaking the machine would only delay him getting home at a normal time.

The sample was calling him the whole time, like it wanted to show off to him. He thought that a few times he could sense something each time he glanced over to it. This is the one, he thought, as he held it up to look at it one more time before the destructive test.

He clamped it in the jig and set the tester. It was spinning quickly and started to pull. The strength meter rose quickly to the set limits, and then went right by them. He had never seen it go this high. It would surely surpass the limits of this test as it rose swiftly past the upper machine limits. The instant before it passed the machine limits, it snapped with a thunderous explosion. The conclusion of the sound wave bounced off the concrete lab walls and reverberated past him again. He removed his earplugs and turned the tester off.

"Whew, almost bought the farm there. That was too bitchin," he said.

He released the two parts out of the jig and set them into the sample box with the other tested pieces. "Amazing," he said, as he picked up the sample, now broken in two. He held it up for a once over. "This is one good run of steel," he said.

He finished his paper work and placed each sample with its specification sheet onto the rack for storage. The triplicate copies went under each sample box as he loaded the samples, one by one, onto the rack. When he got to the super sample, as he called it now in his own mind, he opened the lid to look at it one more time. When he saw the sample, he was quite perplexed. He was sure the destructive test split it in two, but now it was attached at one corner.

Well, maybe he was wrong. Maybe it was still partially attached, he thought. Too strange, but surely he must have been mistaken, because there it was, still attached at a corner, as real as could be. He loaded all the samples onto the cart with the corresponding paper work. He checked the files to be sure they related the steel coils to their clients, and finished up his day.

He stopped the cart at the release supervisor's room. "Here you go," he said to the supervisor. "They all look good to go."

"Alright, thanks," the supervisor responded lackadaisically.

"Yes, you will like this one. There is one coil that is the best. I call it the magical strength coil."

The supervisor looked up and gave him a puzzled look. "You are spending way too much time in that lab. What have you been taking in there? We need to get someone in there to check on you before you get really wonky."

"Oh, yeah? You will see," the technician said.

The coils were set up for release and the corresponding paperwork was filed to document their passing.

Part Four

Chapter Fourteen: Gathering

Miles away, at the house on Carolina, the day was quite gorgeous. The sun was shining above the dew covered grass of the finely trimmed lawn. The house looking seemingly perfect, but it was holding a gravely serious issue. Aricka looked out of her window with dismay. She knew her dad was gone and had to come to accept it. She knew he would find a way to finally come to peace with his life and who he was.

"Hey, Aricka, get ready, they will be here in a few minutes," her mom called from down the hallway.

"Ok, Mom," she replied. She climbed out of bed, leaving the window curtain open, to either let the sun in or to show that she was waiting for him to come home. She left her bedroom door open too as she went down the hallway.

At the entrance to the kitchen, Aricka perked up seeing her mom standing there holding a gleaming necklace. It was beautiful in and of itself. It shone gloriously by the sunlight coursing through the windows. It was truly beautiful. She knew exactly what it was.

"It has been a long time since your dad got this for you," her mom said. "He got it for you years ago. I think you were a small, tiny baby, if I remember right. He wanted to save it to give to you when the day was right. He wanted it to be the most special moment for you to remember, a day you could truly understand how much you were his angel. I think this is that day, so I need to let you have this. Your father was and is always proud of you. You are his saving grace."

She unclasped the necklace and put it around Aricka's neck. The necklace was a sight to behold as it lay gently close to her heart. It gave her resolve to move on with life. The gorgeous pink butterfly necklace on a silver chain helped her find peace immediately.

"Thanks, Dad," she whispered.

The living room was set up with multiple chairs around the edge of the room. A buffet table was against the long wall towards the kitchen doorway. It held some punch, a coffee maker, and some finger sandwiches on one end. The other end was open for the food that others were going to bring.

A gathering at home was all they could do, as the church was not an acceptable place to hold a service. The building had long gone into deterioration with the loss of their pastor. They had not attended another church as it never felt like home. They could not get comfortable in another church and had stopped attending long ago.

The people came in slowly, stopping to hug Aricka and her mother as they entered. The grief was palpable for the family. The mill representative helped them come to terms with their financial needs, since Christian was lost at work. His benefits would be able to cover their daily expenses.

Christian's parents stayed the whole time. Each person at the gathering had nice stories to tell about Christian and his life. They told how he would always help the downtrodden and that he could always be counted on. They talked about how he seemed to be in control each moment of his life. It was a sad day to be losing someone so very young.

Aricka stood steadfast throughout the day. She seemed to hold a silent strength in her. Her mom held it together the best she could. She knew it was meant to be, even though she could not find a way to understand what the plan was, but she had no choice. She missed him terribly.

It was a strange moment as Aricka stood near the kitchen doorway off the living room. The old deacon from the church started up a conversation with her asking about the ability for Christian to maybe be able to see the pastor again.

He wanted to know how he had been lost in Lake Michigan. He wanted to know more about the Bermuda Triangle of the Great Lakes. How did the pastor fall overboard before his sailboat turned up floating aimlessly around the east coast of the lake? Aricka was curious, but deemed it inappropriate to discuss the issue. Her dad was lost in a known accident. The pastor was lost and was never to be found.

"You know, that is what set the church on its path to failure," the old deacon said.

"Yes, my dad told me that story a lot. He really felt at one with that pastor in that church."

"Yes, it was a true tragedy. Maybe now there will be some closure, with your dad up there helping," the deacon said as he smiled.

"Maybe," she replied, knowing in her heart her dad had a lot more to do first before that was to come about.

Chapter Fifteen: Dock

As the sweat is running down your neck
All your praying for to stop you' body breakin' up
Oh your heart is pumping gonna soon explode
Got to fight the horror of this mental load
We are screaming for vengeance
The world is a manacled place
Screaming, screaming for vengeance
The world is defiled in disgrace

-Judas Priest, "Screaming for Vengeance", 1982

The steel coils, now loaded and chained tightly to the flatbed trailer, were ready to go. The semi driver snapped the chains with his hands to make sure they were true and taut. He walked around the trailer one more time to check the load.

"Get on it," the dock loader quipped to him. "You're moving like molasses," he taunted him.

"Oh, hush up you snarly mess. We'll get there, don't worry your little head," the driver quipped back.

The semi driver climbed up into the cab of the truck to get it in gear. It struggled mightily, as the load bore down on the strong diesel engine. Each gear shifted quickly. The load was on its way to the stamping plant.

He really liked this route, as he knew his load would be stamped into the actual steel bodies of the cars. These loads actually became bodies on new cars that people lined up to buy or waited on to come in after they ordered them. He always thought it was quite honorable to deliver the steel coils that would soon become graceful brand new cars.

As he approached the exit, his truck ran better each foot it traveled. It seemed like the oil in the engine was working at its peak performance. He checked in at the security gate. It was the standard minimal check since he had been there so many times before. He knew every security guard. His rapport with each of them was about the same. They would glance at his load out form and then open the gate for him to get to the unloading dock.

He was not sure of the reason he was given a casual wave through the gates. Did they let him through fast because the plant had to have each and every one of the coils for production? Maybe they were smart enough to know, that as a supplier to the third largest auto company in the United States, they had to get things done faster, cheaper, and better than the other two big car manufacturers. They were suppliers to the third in line and it was not even close.

The stamping plant supplied the smallest auto manufacturer, so things were always tense, as if the next order would never come. So maybe the guards knew to keep the supplies flowing for the plant. The faster they could get the raw materials in, the faster they could get the stamped bodies out to assembly. But then again, maybe they just really liked him, he thought.

The truck hustled the coil around the back lot. He turned the wheel tight to back the trailer into the cramped unloading space. He backed up the trailer with great skill. The normal clunk of the trailer smacking the rubber dock stopper was strangely quiet tonight. It was a perfect docking, one in a million. The forklift driver actually stood up as far as he could in the seat of the forklift and clapped for his prowess. He hopped out of the cab to release the chains for the forklift driver.

It was an instant no one saw coming. The chain released suddenly with a crack of a whip. He jumped back, but not quickly enough. The coil rolled dangerously over. The other chain snapped like a dried twig and released the coil. He couldn't move fast enough in the right direction and the coil rocketed past him, clipping his left arm.

The flash of the sharp edge of the steel coil sliced him quickly without him feeling it. He wasn't even aware of what happened, until he felt warm liquid running down his left side. Quickly, he looked down to see his arm now severed off. It lay there on the ground. His arm was sheared cleanly off.

The forklift driver was stunned, but his trained reflexes took over. He leapt off the forklift to hit the large red emergency button. The semi driver fainted immediately, either from seeing his arm lying on the ground or from the severe loss of blood shutting his body down or a combination of both.

It was a split second decision and the forklift operator had the drivers arm stump compressed with a first aid tourniquet. The other workers immediately knew how to respond, as if they were in an instinctive first aid triage. They had his severed arm wrapped and put into a cooler of ice.

The ambulance was moments away and showed up in time to get everything moved to the hospital. The severity of the moment was lost in instant as soon as the ambulance drove away with sirens blaring. The workers all stood there looking at the scene. It was strange for them to take it all in. The coil lay perfectly on the dock, as it had been destined to roll off the trailer and into position to be lifted by the forklift. It was something they had always trained for, a coil getting out of sorts and taking someone's life. The training had prepared them for a wild coil. The resting place of the coil on the dock made no sense though. It should have rolled directly off the trailer bed with gravity dragging it down to the ground.

After a full safety review, the incident was documented as poor technique. The coil was released to production for stamping. The forklift driver hooked the coil to load it onto the take up jig. He removed the specification sheet from the clip. Normally, he would put the spec sheet onto the line clipboard like a robot, but this one was different, so he had to look at it. This was the coil

97

he thought had some strange qualities to it. As he read the testing sheet, he knew something was different. He wasn't trained to know what it said, but he could sure understand the graphs of low to high and good to bad. The graphs showed this coil to be at the top of its testing. This coil was surely something to be reckoned with.

Chapter Sixteen: Production

Delivery went smooth from there out to the stamping plant. The truck docking was flawless. The forklift retrieved the coil from the truck bed and moved it effortlessly in the plant.

"Over here," Moe said and motioned where to go. "Put it in the rack quick, we can't run out of steel today, Bud," he said.

The forklift deftly loaded the coil onto the empty spool. The operator jockeyed it into position and it rolled away.

"Give me a hand over here, Jed!" Moe yelled out. Jed wandered over slowly.

"Hey, you have two speeds there, Boy," Moe said.

"What are you talking about?" Jed shot back. "You're always jacking your mouth with me."

"Oh, yeah? Well, it's your two speeds that set me off. Slow and stop!" Moe retorted.

Jed made his way over to the spool and grabbed the wrench bar to pry the coil around.

"Ok, hold it there. I will grab the end," Moe said.

Jed pried the bar mightily until the coil slowly lurched onto the roller.

"Hold it there, right there," Moe said and pushed the coil end into the first roller of the rubber pinch roller.

"Whoa, good, good, don't let it move while I bump the throttle uptake switch," Moe said.

Jed held tightly, but very carefully. He in no way wanted to be near the razor sharp leading edge of the coil if Moe bumped the throttle switch too much. He had already heard the story of this particular coil. It had a penchant for body parts and he was not going to tempt fate. Moe bumped the switch perfectly and the coil loaded smoothly. Jed jumped back, bar in hand, to let it go. The leading edge moved to align itself with the guide rollers. It was off and running to speed and into the stamping die section.

100

The first part ran easily and stamped the main body parts for the car. The top section, the side sections, and the body pan all came stamped out. Right in a row, the stamped panels rolled off the line from the raw steel coil.

"Looking good," Moe said as he walked by. He loved to watch the stamped parts come from the basic flat coil he loaded. The mega ton die slammed perilously into the raw sheet steel and then rose to leave a perfectly born steel body part. It was ready to become a car for someone to enjoy and cherish, new off the showroom floor. With a wham, each hit of the die into the steel rang out with a thunderous clap.

"Yeah, looks good today!" the operator yelled at Moe over the thunderous pounding.

The machine stamped out parts tirelessly. Each panel churned out of the enormous hydraulically powered stamping die. Just as Moe was turning back to his post on the dock, just before the next load, the machine stopped. Throughout the plant, anyone could have heard a pin drop, seemingly over the standard hydraulic humming of the motors. Moe spun around and instantly returned to the operator station.

"What the heck was that?" Moe asked. "I have never seen that happen."

"Stopped cold in its tracks," the operator said.

"Stopped cold dead," Moe replied.

The machine had set off all of its safety switches. The die struck the steel, but made no action. The steel stood relentless against the die. The control sensor took the lack of relief of the steel as the indicator to shut down. If the steel did not distort to the required depth, the safety switch faulted to off. The die never hit the neutral switch and by default, the hydraulic stamping motor shut down.

"Too cool," Moe said.

"Cool? No way! We need this to keep going. We have a production number to meet. You know we supply the third in line auto manufacturer, so we have to be better, faster, and on time. We could slip into oblivion if the third in line auto maker goes belly up," the operator said.

"Oh, yeah? Well then let's get this thing rolling again!" Moe shouted.

The mechanic was standing next to the control panel in a flash.

"What did you do?" he asked.

"I didn't do anything," the operator said. "It just stopped."

"At this particular point in the roll?" he asked.

"Well yes, at this particular point," the operator said. "Why would I have ever stopped?" he snapped back.

"Oh ok," he said sheepishly, as he was a little guy and the operator was a large, burly guy. He did not want to make him mad. He could crush him with one hand. He was a huge monster of a man.

Moe smiled quickly. He knew exactly what the mechanic was thinking. No one ever messed with the stamping operator. He was built like he could personally stamp out steel parts with one arm.

The mechanic checked the safety switches. Each one passed the test.

"No sign of fault, it should be fine," the mechanic said. "Start it back up."

The operator hit the switch to pull the die up to the top of its travel path.

"Looks good," the mechanic said. "Let it rip."

The motor whirred and the die struck soundly and solidly. The steel creaked and groaned a dreadful groan, but gave way to the force of the die. As the die rose up, the shape that was left was exactly perfect. Moe's eyes were wide with amazement.

"Is that what I think it is?" Moe asked. The operator also looked wide eyed at the part ejected from the die stamper.

"Yes, I think it's the most perfect shape I have ever seen. The detail is spot on," the operator said. "Look, even the finest details are showing up."

"The small radius has smooth edges," Moe said.

"Yes, even the finest tight corners are set exactly," the operator replied.

The stamped body parts sat in line on the conveyor, slowly moving out of the die stamping station to the coater station. Both the operator and Moe watched intently as it left out of sight on the conveyor. They both shrugged their shoulders at each other, and then seemingly forgot what even happened.

Chapter Seventeen: Resilience

The stamped body parts ran through the coater to keep them rust free before they transferred to the welding section of the plant. It was quite a long run along a slow conveyor to the welding stations. Each piece automatically ran into its respective line up jigs to get it set for potion into the welding jig. The welders then tied them together.

The speed of the line was set exactly for each welder to get their weld done as it moved by them. The welders were pros at each weld and had done each weld thousands of times. They worked in unison with symphony type precision. The body was like each one before it. The welders took their time to keep the welds tight exactly along the seams. The conveyor sent the finished welded panels to the quality control station.

Jeff, the quality control weld inspector, looked over his shoulder to see the finished body coming up next. He grinned wildly, as he always liked to start on a new body, even though each one was the same. He really liked starting a new one each time, hoping he would find something different in the next one. He smiled as the body rolled on the conveyor towards him. He gripped the measuring jig, his clipboard, and a weld tester. His experience was nearly legendary. He reveled in trying to find how he could get the welders to do a better job. This one was no different. He always painstakingly checked the potential weak points in the connections for the stamped parts.

Each weld was a story to Jeff. He carefully checked each one. As the line rolled at its normal pace, Jeff found himself rechecking each weld some three times. He was dumbfounded at each check. He scratched his head each time. He even went to the abnormal spots to check the non-critical welds. H was struck and puzzled with amazement.

"This is not possible," he said out loud. "There is no way these welds can be beyond perfection. I can't even tell where there was a weld, if I had known where to check," he kept saying to himself. "There is no way. This is not possible," he repeated.

He had checked every part and then some he would never consider checking, each time shaking his head in disbelief. After spending double the time he was allotted, he gave up, verified the quality checklist as passed, and taped the sheet onto the inside panel.

Break time was far too long a wait for Jeff. He wanted it to come quicker than he could wait. Jeff was usually the last one in the break room, but today he was the first. He looked around and found the table the welders sat at. They were a close bunch who stuck together and didn't care much for outsiders, especially the quality control weld reviewer. Jeff didn't care and went straight away to their table. They all looked up with a grudgingly look. Jeff could see the look on each of their faces. He didn't care. He had to know.

"So, what are you guys up to?" Jeff blurted out.

"Eating some snacks," they said puzzled.

"No really, what did you guys do to that one body? You know what I am talking about."

"Which one?" a welder asked.

"You know, the one you used the new technique on. Did you try, maybe a higher temperature or maybe a longer weld time? Which

109

is it?" Jeff asked, getting increasingly upset. "You guys have to tell me!"

"What are you talking about? Are you feeling ok today?" another welder asked.

"No, you have to tell me! That one had welds that were imperceptible. They were beyond perfect. Those welds could not be discerned from a solid piece of steel. I couldn't find any flaws anywhere."

The welders all perked up and smiled.

"So, you are giving us a compliment?" one of them asked.

"Well, I guess I am," Jeff replied. "Please tell me how did you do it?"

"We are just getting really good," one of them said. "And it's all due to your solid tutelage," he quipped with a smile.

"Yes, your constant nit picking has made us that good," another said and they all laughed out loud.

"Ok guys, you won't tell me, so enough. You don't have to make fun of me," he said.

Jeff walked off in a huff. The welders all cracked up out loud and gave each other high fives.

"I think he has truly lost it now," one said.

"Yes, but it's to our advantage," another said. "Don't make him mad now!"

Jeff had had enough. He went back to his post to check the welds for the next shift.

The body rolled along the line and to the end with a final stop of a crane. The crane lifted the body onto a large trailer jig loaded with other bodies stood up on end to save space. Each one was aligned and ready for plucking off at the assembly plant.

Chapter Eighteen: Assembly - Penance

The trip to the assembly plant was the shortest trip yet. It was just across the back lot to the open bay door. The plant specifically built it in place to reduce the work flow. They were designed and built just in time for the onslaught of the market. There was a veritable boom in production due to demand. A growing economy helped, along with the blooming interstate highway system that brought about a seemingly endless demand for autos.

"What's up, Charlie?" the loader asked. "Step up your pace there," he chided him. "We need to keep the line rolling."

Charlie, the off loader setup transport guy smiled at him with disdain and went about his normal duty and pace. He knew he could only move so fast or something would surely go wrong.

"Hey!" Charlie shouted. "You know I am gonna get it done and done right. You just hold your horses there. You know this one right here is famous and some even say it's possessed with demons. You know something about a steel worker named Christian."

"Oh infamous, you mean," the loader laughed. "You know I am a Christian and don't believe in these random demon things. There is always a reason for everything, even bad things. You just need to listen and pay attention. The answer will be shown to you if you have an open mind," the loader replied.

"You and your open mind. I know I need to be more attentive," Charlie said as he pressed the buttons to load the infamous body onto the assembly hooks. The car body was behind the other bodies that were slowly moving into the assembly process. "You just get the right build sheets onto the right bodies. That is enough for you."

"I got it, I got it, you just get them loaded and hooked so I can do my job. You know you can't name a car Christian. You have to have a female name."

"Ok," Charlie replied. "Then let's name it the female version of Christian."

114

He placed each sheet with the build specifications on each body. It contained everything about the assembled car on it, from the windows, to the carpet type, to the wheel size, to the paint color.

"You see, this one right here is going to be sky blue," he smiled to the other, as he fixed the build sheet onto the inside body panel. "This next one is going to be red burgundy rum."

"So what, I got it. I see it."

"Don't get them mixed up."

"Mixed up? What does it matter? How about I put the red burgundy rum one on the sky blue one? It makes no difference."

"Yeah, you are right. It would not make any difference."

He took the sky blue build sheet and moved it to the one in front of the infamous body and tagged the infamous one with a red burgundy rum color build sheet.

"That wouldn't be Christian," Charlie quipped.

The bodies rolled steadily down the line. Each station added exactly what the build sheet had on it, like the paint color, the wheels, the carpet, and the top. The radio slipped in effortlessly for the line worker. He was simply amazed at how quick it went in, like it wanted to be installed.

He plugged in the connectors and the radio lit up warmly to play a top hit of the time. He was startled and quickly turned the volume knob off. That should not have happened. It's never happened before. Oh well, at least I know it works and is in right, he thought. In an instant he was onto the next car in line.

Chapter Nineteen: Aricka - Peace

Angel eyes
My heart relies
On the love you give to me
You never let me down
You're always by my side
And I'll never, never let you go
I will never let you go
When my heart starts to crumble
And the tears start to fall
You hold me close with tender lovin'
And give me strength to carry on
I'll never let you go
You're always on my mind
You're the only one for me
You're all I need
And I'll never, never let you go

-Steelheart, "I'll Never Let You Go", 1991

Miles away, the sunny warm air wafted into her window. Aricka had not been here in years, let alone decades. She knew the drive well. The location was as familiar to her as the back of her hand. She was older now, but the memories had not faded in any way.

117

She looked at the front of the house and wondered if it could all be true. She was swiping her tablet to look at the articles. One showed the front of the house and an apparition seemed to appear in the window. She knew exactly what it was. She knew the image all too well. She could not find a way to admit it, but she knew it was her dad. He was or had been here.

Aricka knew she had to come back. She had to find a way to know once and for all why there were people calling this place the portal to hell. It could not be. She knew her dad was frustrated, but she also knew he had love in him. He always called her his angel. From her earliest memories, she could sense the good in him being taken over by something he could not control.

The house was not in the best shape, but it wasn't bad either. The owners had kept it up decently. The house was one of normal, blue collar stature. It was a small bungalow of standard proportions of its time.

She remembered the good days with her dad in the yard. He always helped her make everything better. It was this reason she had to come back. She was older now, but she still wondered about her dad.

The stories she read on the tablet were very detailed. She read the details about the watery footsteps in the basement and knew exactly what it was. There were days the basement would get water in it from the high water table and the sump pump stopped working. Her dad would always be down there tinkering with it to get it pumping again.

The current family living there now thought they were being taken over. Aricka knew it was her dad just being himself. He didn't want those kinds of people in his house. His protective side somehow found a way back to protect his house. Somehow he must have been filled with enough desire that he made it back.

The family was happy to rent the nice home and moved in with hopes for a peaceful time. They were looking for a new start in a nice, hard-working neighborhood. From the very first night, though, the house was a quandary. Some light switches would not work all the time and the bulbs would flicker spontaneously. The kids grew testy and the house was heavy with a palpable load on each ones persona.

Long moments just sitting in the car made her wonder if maybe it was all senseless and baseless. Maybe she just wanted it to be true so she could find some closure. The breeze passed through her car effortlessly. The sounds of the now burgeoning neighborhood drifted quietly in the background.

She had a sense of warmth other than that from the sun. It was a sense of compassion, and a feeling of caring she had felt long ago. The sharp sound of gravel startled her and she looked up to see.

In her peripheral vison, she could see in the rearview mirror that there was a car parked behind her now. It was an old burgundy colored car. She did not recognize it, so she thought it must be the owner or the tenant. She waved her hand up in a friendly hello, but as she looked some more, there was no one in there.

Curiously, she looked twice. There was no one there, only just the burgundy car. She felt no fear and pulled the door handle to open the car.

Assuredly, she got out and walked back to the car. There was no one to be found, but the front window was wide open.

She looked around to see if anyone was near. As she tuned back to look into the car, she caught the glimpse of a butterfly rise off the dashboard and out the driver's window. The butterfly circled her and flew over to the house. It landed on the front porch rail and sat there just waving its wings.

Somehow she knew all was at peace. She knew she had found her dad's peace. He had finished his journey to find her one more time. She looked into the car to see a butterfly beanie baby lying in the front seat. It looked just like the one on the necklace she wore every day. There was no doubt in her mind she had to be there that day and she knew the car came to its final destination.

The sun shone brightly on her neck. She was happy to be there. She held the butterfly beanie and her butterfly charm necklace. She said a prayer and thanked the heavens for her dad and the time she was able to have with him. She looked over to the butterfly still sitting peacefully on the porch rail and whispered, "Goodbye. I love you, Daddy."

Epilogue: Carolina - Absolution

Aricka had the weight greater than any amount of steel lifted off her shoulders. She turned the keys for the car ignition. It quickly started up, so she deftly slipped it into drive. She pulled the car onto the pavement to head south, back around to Ridge Road. It was the quickest path to the interstate nowadays. Soon she was whisked into traffic heading north, by way of a quick off ramp to the east.

She knew exactly where she was going. She knew full well her dad would have been proud of her resolve to go and finish college. She would be the first in her family to get a college degree. While she knew the closest campus along her route home was only a satellite campus, it was still a part of the university she would graduate from; plus she knew she wanted to stop there to see the super-sized tricycle.

Her dad would surely have been happy to see the big red tricycle. It was just like the one he bought her when she was very little. She loved that tricycle. She had no doubt that her dad would be drifting alongside her with his newly honored wings. He wouldn't miss the chance to be with her when she saw the tricycle. Maybe it was the article about it that brought her back there in the first place. It was a sign that her dad would never leave her side.

Her phone suddenly lit up. A single bell ringtone chimed from it. Startled, she grabbed the phone up from the passenger seat to see what the notification was, only to find there was nothing. No message, no missed call. No reason whatsoever for the notification ring, let alone that ringtone. She had not programmed that ringtone for anything.

It was a single bell chime. At first she thought it was strange, but then she immediately knew it was her father receiving his wings. She knew he was assuredly now able to be with her whenever she needed him. Aricka smiled and gave a curious wink to her phone as she set it back down on the passenger seat.

"I hear you, Dad," she said smiling.

Made in the USA
San Bernardino, CA
28 September 2014